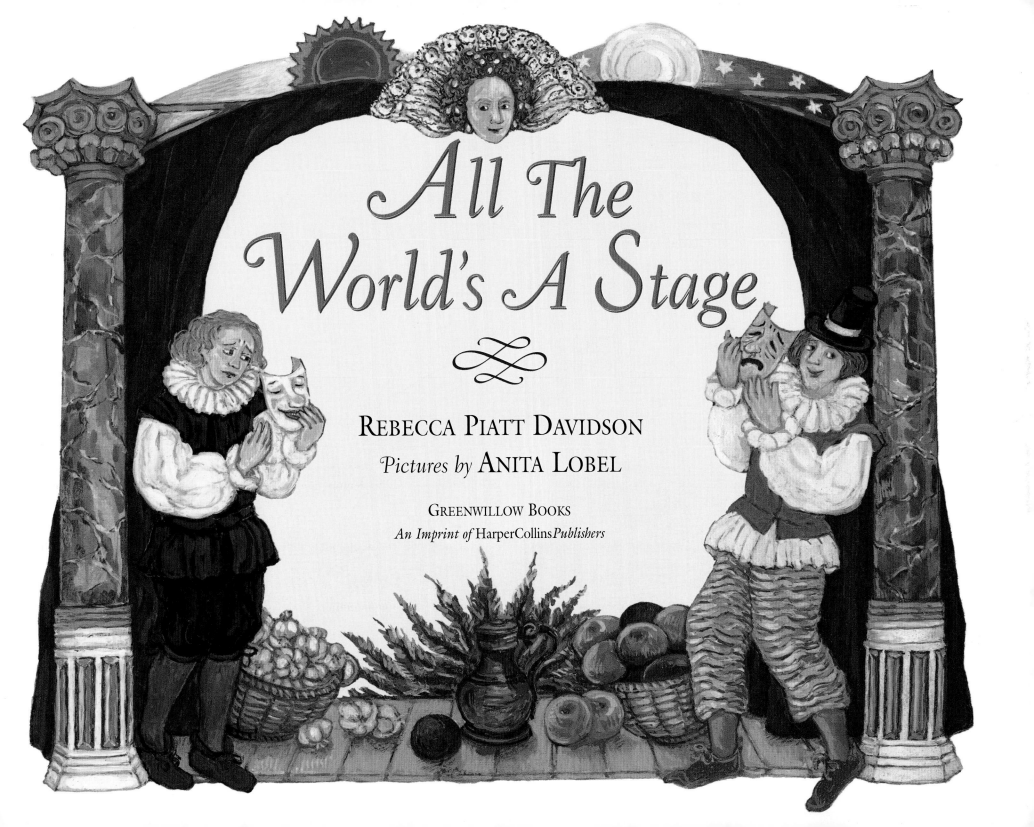

All The World's A Stage

REBECCA PIATT DAVIDSON

Pictures by ANITA LOBEL

GREENWILLOW BOOKS
An Imprint of HarperCollins*Publishers*

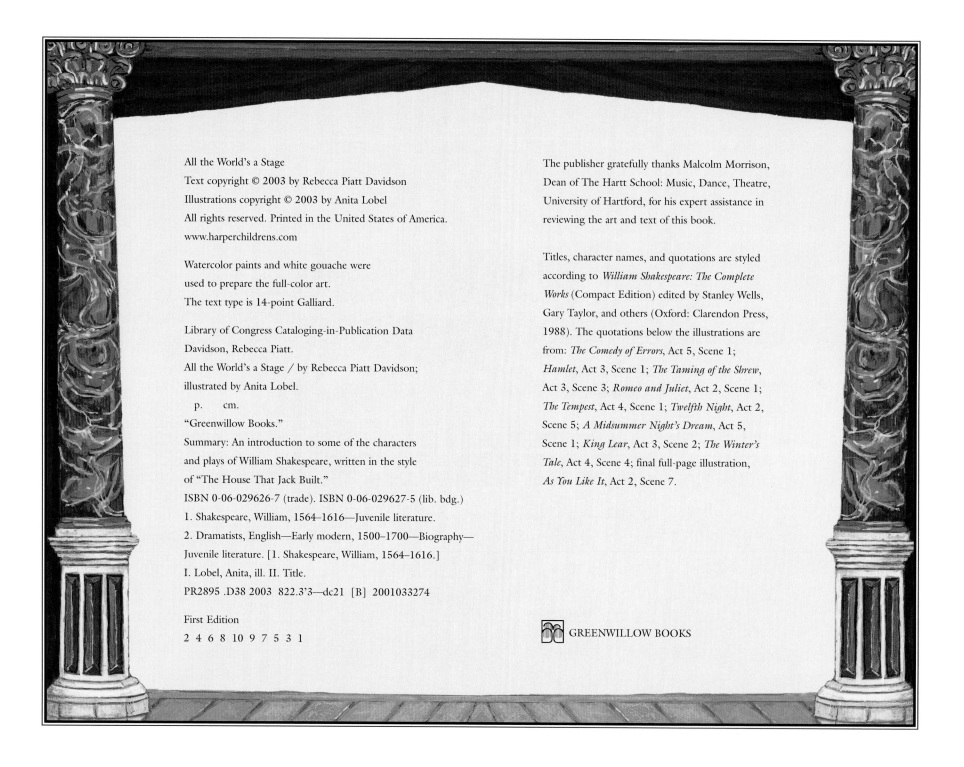

Watercolor paints and white gouache were
used to prepare the full-color art.
The text type is 14-point Galliard.

Library of Congress Cataloging-in-Publication Data

Davidson, Rebecca Piatt.

All the World's a Stage / by Rebecca Piatt Davidson;

illustrated by Anita Lobel.

   p.   cm.

"Greenwillow Books."

Summary: An introduction to some of the characters
and plays of William Shakespeare, written in the style
of "The House That Jack Built."

ISBN 0-06-029626-7 (trade). ISBN 0-06-029627-5 (lib. bdg.)

1. Shakespeare, William, 1564–1616—Juvenile literature.

2. Dramatists, English—Early modern, 1500–1700—Biography—
Juvenile literature. [1. Shakespeare, William, 1564–1616.]

I. Lobel, Anita, ill. II. Title.

PR2895 .D38 2003 822.3'3—dc21 [B] 2001033274

First Edition

2 4 6 8 10 9 7 5 3 1

The publisher gratefully thanks Malcolm Morrison,
Dean of The Hartt School: Music, Dance, Theatre,
University of Hartford, for his expert assistance in
reviewing the art and text of this book.

Titles, character names, and quotations are styled
according to *William Shakespeare: The Complete
Works* (Compact Edition) edited by Stanley Wells,
Gary Taylor, and others (Oxford: Clarendon Press,
1988). The quotations below the illustrations are
from: *The Comedy of Errors*, Act 5, Scene 1;
Hamlet, Act 3, Scene 1; *The Taming of the Shrew*,
Act 3, Scene 3; *Romeo and Juliet*, Act 2, Scene 1;
The Tempest, Act 4, Scene 1; *Twelfth Night*, Act 2,
Scene 5; *A Midsummer Night's Dream*, Act 5,
Scene 1; *King Lear*, Act 3, Scene 2; *The Winter's
Tale*, Act 4, Scene 4; final full-page illustration,
As You Like It, Act 2, Scene 7.

GREENWILLOW BOOKS

For Lynn Dell Simms Piatt (1938–1998),
who is still my Muse . . .
and
Theodore de Valcourt Piatt, Jr.,
longtime storyteller extraordinaire
—R. P. D.

For my own Sweet William, with love,
and for Harold Bloom,
with deep admiration
—A. L.

This is young William,
His mind all ablaze,
Who stays up all night
Writing poems and plays.

This is the Muse
Who sings to the boy
Who stays up all night
Writing poems and plays.

These are the twins
In matching disguises,
Courting and sporting
All kinds of surprises . . .

Amusing the Muse
Who sings to the boy
Who stays up all night
Writing poems and plays.

"We came into the world like brother and brother, and now let's go hand in hand, not one before another."

This is the Prince
Of *To be or not*;
He stops and he goes,
And he's cold and then hot . . .

Confusing the twins
Who amuse the Muse
Who sings to the boy
Who stays up all night
Writing poems and plays.

"To be, or not to be; that is the question."

This is the maiden,
Saucy and smart,
Who battles with words
That are two-edged and tart . . .

Which shocks the Prince
Who confuses the twins
Who amuse the Muse
Who sings to the boy
Who stays up all night
Writing poems and plays.

"I see a woman may be made a fool if she had not a spirit to resist."

These are the children
Who pledge secret love,
Ignoring the signs
Of the stars up above . . .

Which hushes the maiden
Who shocks the Prince
Who confuses the twins
Who amuse the Muse
Who sings to the boy
Who stays up all night
Writing poems and plays.

"What's in a name? That which we call a rose by any other word would smell as sweet."

This is the Duke
And his airy sprite,
Who work their magic
One stormy night . . .

Enchanting the children
Who hush the maiden
Who shocks the Prince
Who confuses the twins
Who amuse the Muse
Who sings to the boy
Who stays up all night
Writing poems and plays.

"We are such stuff as dreams are made on."

*T*his is the servant
In bright yellow tights,
Who foolishly longs
For the Countess in white . . .

Who fears the Duke
Who enchants the children
Who hush the maiden
Who shocks the Prince
Who confuses the twins
Who amuse the Muse
Who sings to the boy
Who stays up all night
Writing poems and plays.

"Some are born great, some achieve greatness, and some have greatness thrust upon 'em."

These are the fairies
Whose mischief delights
All the woodfolk who witness
Their fanciful flights . . .

And inspires the servant
In bright yellow tights,
Who longs for the Countess
Who fears the Duke
Who enchants the children
Who hush the maiden
Who shocks the Prince
Who confuses the twins
Who amuse the Muse
Who sings to the boy
Who stays up all night
Writing poems and plays.

"Think . . . you have but slumbered here, while these visions did appear."

These are the daughters,
Always in fights
Over what is whose kingdom
And who has first rights,
Robbing their King of
His good, trusty knights . . .

Which saddens the fairies
Who inspire the servant
Who longs for the Countess
Who fears the Duke
Who enchants the children
Who hush the maiden
Who shocks the Prince
Who confuses the twins
Who amuse the Muse
Who sings to the boy
Who stays up all night
Writing poems and plays.

"I am a man more sinned against than sinning."

This is the statue
Of a Queen, fair and bright,
Who comes back to life,
Saying, "All is made right!"
She embraces her King,
Whose heart is contrite. . . .

"I think there is not half a kiss to choose who loves another best."

And he bows to his lady,
Who bows to the daughters,
Who bow to the fairies,
Who bow to the servant,
Who bows to the Countess,
Who bows to the Duke,
Who bows to the children,
Who bow to the maiden,
Who bows to the Prince,
Who bows to the twins,
Who bow to the Muse,
Who bows to young William,
Who stands and declares,

"You'll be my players
And the world, my stage.
We'll live through the tales
That unfold on each page!
Happy you'll be
When you act well your part,
And happier, I,
Making words into art."

"All the world's a stage, and all the men and women merely players."

William Shakespeare (1564–1616) was a sometime actor and poet-playwright in England during the reign of Queen Elizabeth I. Little is known of his early years in the market town of Stratford-upon-Avon. When he was eighteen, he married Anne Hathaway, with whom he had three children: Susanna, and twins Judith and Hamnet.

It is not known how and why Shakespeare came to reside in London. Once there, however, he began working in the theater, first as an actor on the stage and then as a playwright. His fame grew, and he eventually became a shareholder in the Globe Theatre.

William Shakespeare is credited with writing thirty-seven plays and more than one hundred poems, as well as with creating some of the most memorable characters in world literature.

A NOTE FROM THE ILLUSTRATOR

My many years of involvement with theater, as a spectator and sometime performer, have directly influenced my career in picture books. I've always treated texts as if they were little staged dramas in need of scenery and costumes, populated with characters who gesture and amuse as if they were actors on the stage.

How perfect, then, to have the chance to create paintings for this narrative about some plays and players from the works of Shakespeare. I loved designing costumes and masks, marble-painted columns, backdrops with images of stormy seas or night skies, and red draperies on a string that an invisible hand might pull across the back of the stage for a change of scene.

When I envisioned the paintings for *All the World's a Stage*, I wanted to open the book by formally introducing young William Shakespeare and his muse with individual portraits. From there the cumulative rhyming text led me to present on the left-hand pages the many characters springing from William's mind and quill. On the right-hand pages I staged a kind of group portrait of characters from each play. These pictures are not meant to represent actual scenes. Rather, they are composites that highlight key dramatic moments from the plays.

–Anita Lobel

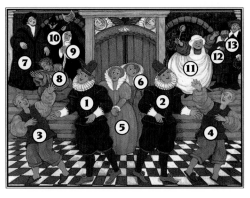

❧ THE COMEDY OF ERRORS ❧

*T*wo sets of identical twins cause comic confusion when, twenty years after being separated at birth, they unknowingly end up in the town of Syracuse.

CAST OF CHARACTERS

1. & 2. Antipholus of Ephesus and Antipholus of Syracuse—twin sons of Egeon and Emilia but unknown to each other

3. & 4. Dromio of Ephesus and Dromio of Syracuse—twin brothers and attendants of the two Antipholuses

5. Adriana—wife of Antipholus of Ephesus

6. Luciana—Adriana's sister

7. Solinus—Duke of Ephesus

8. Egeon—a merchant of Syracuse and the duke's captive

9. Emilia—wife of Egeon, disguised as an abbess

10. & 11. A jailer and a cook

12. Angelo—a goldsmith

13. Balthasar—a merchant

❧ HAMLET ❧

THE TRAGEDY OF HAMLET,
PRINCE OF DENMARK

*H*amlet is determined to avenge his father's death, but his grief and murderous anger push him to the brink of madness.

CAST OF CHARACTERS

1. Hamlet—son of the former king of Denmark and nephew of the present king
2. Horatio—Hamlet's friend
3. Ghost of Hamlet's father
4. Ophelia—daughter of Polonius
5. Polonius—Lord Chamberlain
6. Laertes—son of Polonius
7. Claudius—King of Denmark and Hamlet's uncle
8. Gertrude—Queen of Denmark and Hamlet's mother
9. The Player King and Queen
10. Rosencrantz and Guildenstern—courtiers
11. Gravediggers

❧ THE TAMING OF THE SHREW ❧

*F*iery-tempered Katherine meets her match when she is forced to marry the swaggering Petruccio. A game of wits ends in mutual respect between two strong-willed people.

CAST OF CHARACTERS

1. Katherine—elder daughter of Baptista
2. Petruccio—a gentleman from Verona and Katherine's suitor
3. Bianca—Katherine's younger sister (with two of her suitors)
4. Baptista—a rich gentleman of Padua and father of Katherine and Bianca (with two more suitors)

❧ ROMEO AND JULIET ❧

THE MOST EXCELLENT AND LAMENTABLE
TRAGEDY OF ROMEO AND JULIET

*I*gnoring the long-standing feud between their families, young Romeo and Juliet fall in love and marry. But their hopes and plans go awry and end in tragedy.

CAST OF CHARACTERS

1. Romeo, son of Lord Montague of Verona
2. Juliet, daughter of Lord Capulet of Verona
3. Juliet's nurse
4. Friar Laurence—a monk
5. & 6. Lord and Lady Capulet
7. Paris—a young nobleman
8. Mercutio—Romeo's friend
9. A youth of the Montague family
10. Tybalt—Juliet's cousin
11. A youth of the Capulet family

❧ THE TEMPEST ❧

*P*rospero, the vengeful, maligned Duke of Milan, is shipwrecked on a magical island, where he is transformed by the mercy he shows others.

CAST OF CHARACTERS

1. Prospero—the rightful Duke of Milan, now a magician
2. Ariel—an airy spirit serving Prospero
3. Caliban—a savage and deformed slave of Prospero
4. Stephano—a butler
5. Trinculo—a jester
6. Ferdinand—son of Alonso, the king of Naples
7. Miranda—Prospero's daughter
8. Antonio—Prospero's brother, now Duke of Milan
9. & 10. Adrian and Francisco—lords in the court
11. Sebastian—King Alonso's brother
12. Gonzalo—a counselor in the court

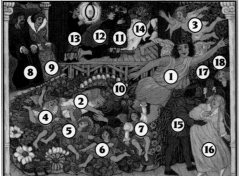

❧ TWELFTH NIGHT ❧

or WHAT YOU WILL

The arrogant and foolish steward Malvolio is tricked by the household of the Countess Olivia in this comedy of mistaken identities.

CAST OF CHARACTERS

1. Malvolio—Olivia's servant

2. Olivia—a countess

3. Viola—a young woman, dressed in man's clothing, who serves Duke Orsino

4. Orsino—Duke of Illyria

5. Maria—Olivia's maid

6. Sir Toby Belch—Olivia's uncle

7. Sir Andrew Aguecheek—a friend of Sir Toby

8. Feste—a clown-musician who serves Duke Orsino

9. Sebastian—Viola's twin brother, with friends

❧ A MIDSUMMER NIGHT'S DREAM ❧

Oberon, King of the Fairies, and his servant, Puck, weave spells that leave a group of lovers enchanted and hilariously confused.

CAST OF CHARACTERS

1. Oberon—King of the Fairies

2. Titania—Queen of the Fairies

3. Puck, or Robin Goodfellow— servant to Oberon

4., 5., 6. & 7. Other fairies

8. Theseus—Duke of Athens

9. Hippolyta—Queen of the Amazons, engaged to Theseus

10. Bottom—a weaver changed by Oberon into an ass

11. Flute, playing a wall

12. Snug, playing Pyramus

13. Starveling, playing moonshine

14. Snout, playing a lion

15., 16., 17. & 18. The mixed-up lovers: Lysander, Hermia, Demetrius, Helena

❧ KING LEAR ❧

THE TRAGEDY OF KING LEAR

Two of King Lear's daughters, Goneril and Regan, fight to control their aging father's kingdom, while the youngest sister, Cordelia, remains devoted to her father.

CAST OF CHARACTERS

1. Lear—King of Britain

2. The king's fool, or jester

3. Edgar—son of Gloucester

4. & 5. Goneril and Regan— daughters of King Lear

6. Edmond—son of Gloucester

7. Cordelia—youngest daughter of King Lear

8. King of France—Cordelia's husband

9. Gloucester—an earl

10. Kent—an earl

11. Knights

❧ THE WINTER'S TALE ❧

Once a living queen who has been turned to a statue, Hermione is brought back to life through King Leontes's repentance and has the opportunity to meet her long-lost daughter, Perdita.

CAST OF CHARACTERS

1. Leontes—King of Sicily

2. Hermione—Queen of Sicily

3. Paulina—wife of Antigonus and servant to the queen

4. Antigonus—a Sicilian lord

5. Perdita as a baby—daughter of Leontes and Hermione

6. Florizel—son of Polixenes

7. Perdita as a young woman

8. Autolycus—a peddler

9. A shepherd

10. Clown

11. & 12. Mopsa and Dorcas— two shepherdesses

13. Cleomenes—a Sicilian lord

14. Polixenes—King of Bohemia